I'm Taller Than You!

 Crabtree Publishing Company
www.crabtreebooks.com
1-800-387-7650

PMB 16A, 350 Fifth Ave.
Suite 3308,
New York, NY

616 Welland Ave.
St. Catharines, ON
L2M 5V6

Published by Crabtree Publishing in 2008

Series Editor: Jackie Hamley
Series Advisor: Dr. Hilary Minns
Series Designer: Peter Scoulding
Proofreader: Reagan Miller

Text © A. H. Benjamin 2006
Illustration © O'Kif 2006

The rights of the author and the illustrator
of this Work have been asserted.

First published in 2006
by Franklin Watts
(A division of Hachette
Children's Books)

Printed in the U.S.A.—CG

For Isabelle—A.H.B

**Library and Archives Canada
Cataloguing in Publication**

Benjamin, A. H., 1950-
    I'm taller than you! / A.H. Benjamin ;
O'Kif, illustrator.

(Tadpoles)
ISBN 978-0-7787-3854-1 (bound).
--ISBN 978-0-7787-3885-5 (pbk.)

    1. Readers (Primary). 2. Readers--Stature.
3. Readers--Giraffe. I. O'Kif II. Title. III. Series:
Tadpoles (St. Catharines, Ont.)

PE1117.T33 2008n   428.6   C2007-907417-0

**Library of Congress
Cataloging-in-Publication Data**

Benjamin, A. H., 1950-
  I'm taller than you! / by A.H. Benjamin ;
illustrated by O'Kif.
      p. cm. -- (Tadpoles)
    Summary: The other animals are tired of Giraffe
always telling them that he is taller than they are, so
they band together to try and teach Giraffe a lesson.
    ISBN-13: 978-0-7787-3854-1 (reinforced lib. bdg.)
    ISBN-10: 0-7787-3854-X (reinforced lib. bdg.)
    ISBN-13: 978-0-7787-3885-5 (pbk.)
    ISBN-10: 0-7787-3885-X (pbk.)
    [1. Size--Fiction. 2. Animals--Fiction.] I. O'Kif, ill.
II. Title. III. Title: I am taller than you. IV. Series.
PZ7.B43457Iam 2008
    [E]--dc22

                                    2007049216

I'm Taller Than You!

by A. H. Benjamin

Illustrated by O'Kif

Crabtree Publishing Company

www.crabtreebooks.com

A.H. Benjamin

"When I was young I was taller than all my friends. They used to call me Giraffe!"

O'Kif

"When I started drawing this book, I asked myself how things might look from above. I think they probably look very different!"

"I'm taller than you," Giraffe says to Tortoise.

"I'm taller than you,"
Giraffe says to Monkey.

"I'm taller than you,"
Giraffe says to Hyena.

9

"I'm taller than you,"
Giraffe says to Zebra.

"I'm taller than you,"
Giraffe says to Hippo.

"I'm taller than you,"
Giraffe says to Elephant.

"I'm taller than *all* of you!" Giraffe says to everyone.

"No you're not," they all shout.

"We are taller than you!"

But they are not
taller for long!

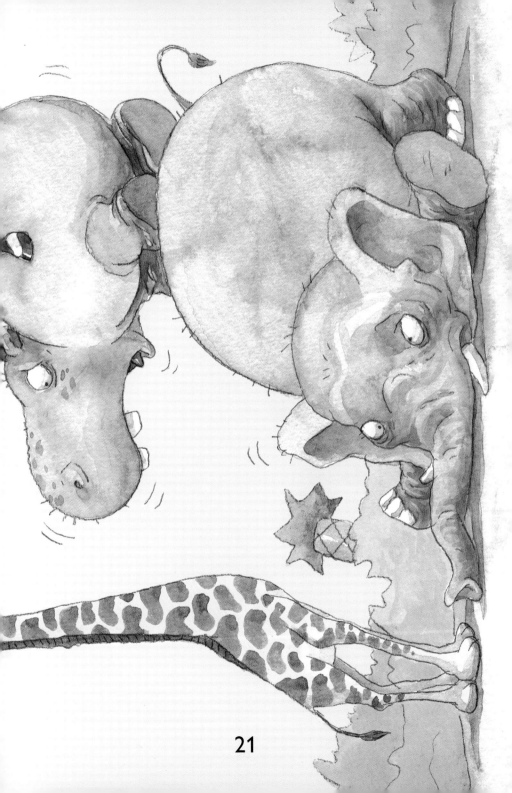

21

"I'm taller than you!" says Giraffe.

23

Notes for adults

TADPOLES are structured to provide support for early readers. The stories may also be used by adults for sharing with young children.

Starting to read alone can be daunting. **TADPOLES** help by providing visual support and repeating high frequency words and phrases. These books will both develop confidence and encourage reading and rereading for pleasure.

If you are reading this book with a child, here are a few suggestions:

1. Make reading fun! Choose a time to read when you and the child are relaxed and have time to share the story.
2. Talk about the story before you start reading. Look at the cover and the blurb. What might the story be about? Why might the child like it?
3. Encourage the child to reread the story, and to retell the story in their own words, using the illustrations to remind them what has happened.
4. Discuss the story and see if the child can relate it to their own experiences, or perhaps compare it to another story they know.
5. Give praise! Children learn best in a positive environment.